James Stevenson

HOWARD

Greenwillow Books   New York

jE

Published by Greenwillow Books
A Division of William Morrow & Company, Inc.
105 Madison Avenue, New York, N.Y. 10016
Design by Ava Weiss
Printed in the United States of America
First Edition
10 9 8 7 6 5 4 3 2 1

Library of Congress Cataloging in Publication Data
Stevenson, James (date)   Howard.
Summary: Because he has missed the annual migration,
Howard the duck spends the winter in New York City.
[1. Ducks—Fiction.   2. New York (City)—Fiction]
I. Title.   PZ7.S84748Ho   [E]   79-16562
ISBN 0-688-80255-9   ISBN 0-688-84255-0 lib. bdg.

It was time to go south for the winter.
"Where's Howard?" said the grown-up ducks.
"We can't wait any longer."

When Howard came out of the woods,
all the ducks were gone.

"Where did the ducks go?" he asked the rabbits.
"Up in the air," said one.
"I know that," said Howard.
"Then they turned left," said the other.

Howard flew up in the air and turned left.

After a few hours, it began to snow.
Howard couldn't see.

He flew down until he saw a place to land.

He was so tired he went right to sleep.

Howard woke up on a roof.
He looked over the edge.
He didn't see any ducks.

When it got dark, Howard flew down to the street.
He saw a cat.
"Pardon me," said Howard. "Is this south?"
"No, stupid," said the cat. "This is New York City."

It was so cold Howard had to keep walking.
"I wonder which way is south," he said to himself.

"Hey, Mac," said a voice. "Are you a pigeon?"
"No," said Howard. "I'm a duck."
"I don't like pigeons," said the frog. "Come on in."
"Is it warm in there?" asked Howard.
"Warmer than the street," said the frog.

"First visit to the
  big city?" he asked.
"Yes," said Howard.

"I'll give you a sightseeing tour of New York,"
said the frog. "Hop aboard. My name is Rex."

"Directly overhead is Radio City Music Hall,"
said Rex, after a while.

"Where are we now?" asked Howard.
"Under the Empire State Building," said Rex.
"World's third tallest building!"

"Thanks for the tour, Rex," said Howard.
"Come back again," said Rex, "and I'll
   show you the World Trade Center."

Howard was very hungry.
He saw some crumbs, and he started to eat them.

Along came a bunch of pigeons.
"Hey! Those are *our* crumbs!"
"This is pigeon territory!"
"Shove off!"

Howard walked on. "I sure could use some shut-eye," he thought. "But where?"

"What's the matter? No place to stay?" said a small voice. "Come on in."

"I'm Hollis," said one mouse.
"That's Wallace, and he's Albert."
"How do you do?" said Howard.
He crawled in.
"Sleep tight," they said, and went to sleep.

But in the morning…

"I forgot this was garbage day," said Hollis.
"It was nice while it lasted," said Howard.

They looked everywhere for somewhere to stay.

"Hey! Watch your step!"
"Sorry," said Howard. "I was looking
   for a warm place."

"Don't get your hopes up," said the dog.
"Nobody has one."

They went down an alley. "Too bad we can't get in this building," said Howard.
"It's been locked for years," said Hollis.

"Maybe there's a way," said Howard. "Let's take a look at the roof."

Howard gave them a ride up.

There was a broken window in the skylight.
"I'll take a look-see," said Wallace. He disappeared.
After a while he called, "Come on down!"

"This is great!" said Howard.
"Plenty of room for everybody!" said Hollis.

They went and told all the cold animals.
"Come on! We've got a place to stay!"
All the animals moved in.

"We can stay here all winter!" said Hollis.
"Darn right!" said Albert.

Every night they had a different show.
One night the cockroaches danced.

The months went by ... but...

One morning, everybody woke up
to a terrible noise.

There was a big hole in the wall.
Men were knocking the building down.

They went outside and saw a sign.
"That doesn't include us," said Albert.

They watched for a while.
Then they walked away.
"Nothing lasts forever," said Wallace.
"Especially in New York."

"At least it's warm now," said Hollis.
"We can sleep outside."
"And we can see all the sights, too!"
 said Albert.

Every day they saw different things.
They went on the subway

and to the museum.

Every night they slept in different places.

One day Howard took everybody
flying over the city so they could see
how everything looked from the top.
"Wow!" said Rex.

Early one morning, they heard quacking.
"That's my group!" said Howard.

Howard took off.
"Gee," said Wallace. "He didn't even say good-bye."
"I guess ducks like ducks," said Hollis.

"It was a nice friendship while it lasted,"
said Albert.
"Nothing lasts forever," said Wallace.
"Especially in New York… "

Suddenly Howard was back.

"Did you come to say good-bye?" asked Rex.

"No, I already said good-bye," said Howard.

"Good-bye to the ducks!"